A Teddy Bear for President Roosevelt

by Peter and Connie Roop
illustrated by Rebecca Thornburgh

SCHOLASTIC INC.

New York   Toronto   London   Auckland   Sydney
Mexico City   New Delhi   Hong Kong   Buenos Aires

For Heidi and Grandpa, who shared many special bear hugs
—P.R. & C.R.

For Alice, and her beloved "Ted the Head"
—R.McK.T.

Photo Credits
p. 7: THE GRANGER COLLECTION, New York; p.11: Library of Congress;
p. 23: Scholastic Photo Archive; p.25: Corbis; p.31: THE GRANGER COLLECTION,
New York; p. 32: Brown Brothers.

ISBN 0-439-44174-9

Copyright © 2002 by Peter and Connie Roop

All rights reserved. Published by Scholastic Inc.
SCHOLASTIC and associated logos are trademarks and/or
registered trademarks of Scholastic Inc.

12 11 10 9 8 7 6 5 4 3 2 1   2 3 4 5 6 7/0

Printed in the U.S.A.
First Scholastic printing, November 2002

"Good-bye, Susan. Good-bye, Franklin," said Mr. Michtom. He closed the door of Michtoms' Candy and Toy Shop. The brass bell over the door jingled merrily.

Susan and Franklin waved good-bye as they ran to school. They thought Mr. and Mrs. Michtom made the best candy in Brooklyn.

Mrs. Michtom carried a tray of candy canes. She had just made them. The small store smelled delicious, like peppermint, chocolate, licorice, lemon, and orange all mixed together.

Mr. Michtom opened his newspaper. He spread it on the counter. The shop door opened. A tall man stomped in and slammed the door.

"Are you reading the newspaper again, Michtom?" Mr. Walker snapped. "You'll never be a good businessman."

"Good morning, Mr. Walker," said Mr. Michtom. "Reading the newspaper every day helps me learn English better."

"That may be. But if you read the newspaper less and sold more candy and toys, you would have the rent money you owe me. Today is November 22, 1902. If you do not pay the rent by January 1, 1903, then out you go."

Mrs. Michtom sputtered, "But, Mr. Walker...we are only one month behind in the rent. This small shop is all we have."

"We owe you only thirty dollars," Mr. Michtom said.

Mr. Walker snatched up a newspaper. He threw a penny onto the counter.

"I will be back on January 1 for my thirty dollars' rent money. Every penny of it!"
Mr. Walker yanked the door open and left.
The bell jangled.

"I would like to smack that man with his newspaper," Mrs. Michtom said when the door closed.

"Now, Mama," Mr. Michtom said calmly, "Mr. Walker is trying to be a good American businessman."

"Papa, you are a good American businessman, too."

"Yes, but I sell only candy, toys, and newspapers. He sells buildings."

"But, Papa, if we are forced out, where will we go?"

Mr. Michtom shook his head. He had no answer. He turned back to his newspaper.

Mrs. Michtom wrapped a candy cane in wax paper.

"Mama," Mr. Michtom said suddenly. "Look at this. Our President Theodore Roosevelt saved the life of a baby bear in the woods."

DRAWING
THE LINE
IN MISSISSIPPI

In 1902, this cartoon appeared in newspapers all over the country. It shows President Theodore Roosevelt refusing to shoot a baby bear.

Mrs. Michtom looked at the picture in the newspaper.

"Oh, Papa, President Theodore Roosevelt loves the little bears just as we loved our Mishka bears back in Russia."

Papa smiled. He remembered his furry toy Mishka bear. His mama had given it to him when he was five years old. He wondered where his Mishka bear was this sad day.

Chapter Two

Mr. Michtom folded his newspaper. He left it open to the picture of President Roosevelt and the bear he had spared.

"Mama, today we are going to make a bear like the one in the newspaper. We will put our bear in the store window. That will show everyone how much we love America, our new country."

"But, Papa, what about Mr. Walker's rent money?"

Mr. Michtom smiled. "When people see what good Americans we are, they will buy more candy and toys from us. Then we will have the rent money."

Mrs. Michtom grinned. "I have a fine piece of furry fabric I was saving to make toy dogs," she said. "It is brown like a bear's fur. I also have shiny black buttons I can sew on for his eyes."

"Let's get to work, Mama," Mr. Michtom said. He picked up his pencil.

Mrs. Michtom spread her fabric on the counter. Mr. Michtom traced the shape of a bear on a piece of paper. He drew a body, a head, two ears, two arms, two legs, and four paws. Mrs. Michtom gently placed the pattern over the fabric and pinned it down. Ever so carefully, she cut out the shape of a bear.

"We can stuff it with straw," Mr. Michtom said.

All day, Mr. and Mrs. Michtom worked on their bear. They stopped only when a customer came in to buy candy. No one bought a toy all day.

By evening, the bear was finished.

Mama held up the bear for Papa to admire.

"What shall we call him?" she asked.

"Mishka," suggested Mr. Michtom.

"No," said Mrs. Michtom. "That is a Russian name. We are Americans now."

Mr. Michtom's eyes fell on his open newspaper. "In honor of our President Theodore Roosevelt, we will name him Theodore Bear."

Theodore Roosevelt was President of the United States from 1901 to 1909.

The Michtoms placed Theodore Bear in their shop window. Mr. Michtom cut out the picture of President Roosevelt and his bear from the paper. He placed the picture beside Theodore Bear.

"Now everyone will know we are Americans!" exclaimed Mr. Michtom.

Chapter Three

The next morning, Susan and Franklin burst into the store.

"Oh, Mr. and Mrs. Michtom. He is beautiful!" Susan exclaimed.

"Who is beautiful besides you this fine day?" asked Mr. Michtom. His eyes twinkled.

"The bear in the window. May I hold him, please?" Susan begged.

Mrs. Michtom picked up the bear. She handed him to Susan. Susan hugged the bear. She handed the bear to Franklin, who squeezed him, too.

"Can we buy him?" Franklin asked.

Mr. Michtom looked at Mrs. Michtom. She shook her head.

But Mr. Michtom saw the look of love in Susan's eyes.

"Yes, for you, my children, Theodore Bear is for sale."

Mrs. Michtom coughed loudly, but Mr. Michtom did not look at her.

"How much is he?" Franklin asked.

Mr. Michtom scratched his head. "For such good customers as you, I say ninety-nine cents."

Franklin looked at Susan. "I have my penny for candy today," he said.

"And I have mine," Susan said. "But that is all we have."

"We can give you our candy money from Grandmama every day until we reach ninety-nine cents," Franklin offered.

Mr. Michtom scratched his head.

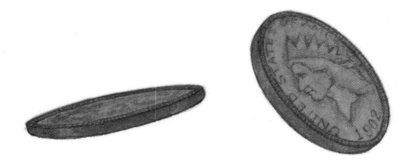

"I tell you what. Theodore Bear is yours. Give me two cents today. Each day when you come, you can pay two more cents. Then you can tell me how Theodore Bear is behaving himself."

The children each gave Mr. Michtom a penny.

"Thank you, thank you!" they cried.

Even Mrs. Michtom smiled when she saw how happy Theodore Bear made Susan and Franklin.

"Theodore sounds too grown-up," said Susan. "I think we should call the bear Teddy, like our friend Theodore at school."

"Come on, Teddy Bear," Franklin shouted.

Susan, Franklin, and Teddy Bear dashed out the door. The bell jingled happily.

Chapter Four

"Oh, Papa," said Mama. "Your heart is too big. Now we have no bear in our window to bring in customers. What happened to my American businessman?"

"But did you not see how they loved our little Theodore Bear, I mean, Teddy Bear?" he asked.

"I did," Mrs. Michtom answered. "But, Papa, we must still pay the rent."

"Do you have any furry fabric left, Mama?" Mr. Michtom asked. He held up the bear pattern. Mrs. Michtom smiled.

"Yes, Papa, I do. And I have many more shiny black buttons, too." Papa picked up the scissors. He said, "Let us then make many more Teddy Bears."

"These we will sell for five dollars each," Mama said sternly.

"Yes, Mama," Mr. Michtom replied meekly.

Each night, the Michtoms made a new bear.
Each day, they sold it. They sold more candy, too.
Soon they had the $30 they needed for Mr.
Walker's rent money. Mrs. Michtom put the $30 in
a special spot in the cash register drawer. With the
rest of their money the Michtoms bought more
furry fabric and more shiny black buttons.

"Papa, you are a good American businessman!"
Mrs. Michtom said proudly.

Each school day, Susan and Franklin paid their two pennies.

Each day, the brass bell over the door jingled merrily.

Until the day Mr. Walker returned.

He entered Michtoms' Candy and Toy Shop. The bell jangled.

Mr. Walker did not even say good morning.

"I am here for my rent money," he grumbled.

Mrs. Michtom opened the cash register. She took out the $30 they had saved.

She handed the money to Mr. Walker.

"But, but, but," Mr. Walker sputtered, "how did you get the money?"

"You see? I, too, am a good American businessman," Mr. Michtom said proudly.

"Well, you won't be for long," Mr. Walker growled. "Not if you keep making fun of President Roosevelt with that silly bear in the window."

Mr. Walker stormed from the store. The bell jangled good riddance.

"Oh, Papa!" exclaimed Mrs. Michtom. "Will we be arrested by the President?"

"I do not think so," Mr. Michtom said sadly. "But we must not make any more Teddy Bears."

Mrs. Michtom frowned. "I do not think such a good man as Mr. Roosevelt minds if we make our bears and give them his name. After all, he did not shoot that poor little bear in the newspaper picture."

"Yes, Mama, you may be right. This is America. But we cannot take any chances. We do not want to be sent back to Russia."

"But then we will be forced out by Mr. Walker because we will no longer have the money from selling our Teddy Bears. We will not be able to pay the rent."

"I will think of something, Mama," Mr. Michtom promised. But he did not know what.

Mrs. Michtom took the Teddy Bear out of the window. She sadly carried him to the back room.

Teddy Roosevelt became President when he was 42 years old. He was the youngest President in the history of the United States.

Chapter Five

The next morning, Susan and Franklin came in with their two cents.

"Why is there no Teddy Bear in the window?" Susan asked.

"We can no longer sell our Teddy Bears," said Mr. Michtom.

"Why not?" Franklin asked.

"Because Mr. President Teddy Roosevelt will not like us naming our bear after him."

"How do you know?" Franklin asked.

"We do not know," Mrs. Michtom said. "But it is not polite to make fun of the President of the United States."

"But you are not making fun," Susan protested. "I bet his daughter Sally would love a Teddy Bear of her own," she added.

"Do you really think so?" asked Mr. Michtom.

"We love our bear," Franklin said, as if he knew all children would love Teddy Bears of their own.

Teddy Roosevelt loved nature. While he was President, he created 5 national parks and 150 national forests!

"If we sent a letter with the Teddy Bear asking President Roosevelt if we could use his name, do you think that would be good?" Mrs. Michtom asked.

"Oh, yes," Susan said. "President Lincoln grew his beard because a little girl asked him to. I am sure President Roosevelt will let you use his nickname, Teddy."

Mrs. Michtom went into the back room. She returned with their last Teddy Bear. She handed him to Franklin and went to get a box.

Mr. Michtom sat down, picked up his best piece of writing paper, and began writing.

When he finished, Mr. Michtom asked, "Where should I send our letter?"

Susan answered, "To President Theodore Roosevelt, The White House, Washington, D.C."

Mr. Michtom wrote the address in big, bold letters on the package.

"Mama, you and the children take the Teddy Bear for President Roosevelt to the post office. I will mind the shop."

With Susan carefully carrying the Teddy Bear package, the three left Michtoms' Candy and Toy Shop.

Every morning, Susan and Franklin ran to the Michtoms' store. Every morning, they paid their pennies. Every morning, they went home sad because no letter had come from President Roosevelt.

"It is only two weeks before we must have the rent money again," Mrs. Michtom said one day.

Mr. Michtom shook his head. "I knew so great a man as President Roosevelt would not have time to write us. But I hope his daughter Sally likes her Teddy Bear."

The door opened.

"Mr. and Mrs. Michtom," said Mr. North, the mailman. "You have a letter from the White House!"

Mr. Michtom's hand trembled as he took the letter.

"Hurry," Mama exclaimed. "Open it!"

"Not until Franklin and Susan come."

Just then, the bell over the door jingled. In ran Susan and Franklin.

"President Roosevelt's letter came!" Susan shouted. "I can tell by your smiles."

Mr. Michtom held up the letter. Ever so carefully, he opened it.

He unfolded the letter and read,

Dear Mr. and Mrs. Michtom,

Sally simply adores her Teddy Bear. She sleeps with it every night. Mrs. Roosevelt and I thank you most sincerely for your kind gift.

As for using my name, you are welcome to it. I do not know what good it may do you, but if it helps bring joy to any child who has one of your Teddy Bears, it is yours to use.

Sincerely yours,

Teddy Roosevelt,
President of the United States

"Hooray!" shouted Susan.
"Hooray!" shouted Franklin.
"Hip! Hip! Hooray!" shouted Mr. North.

"Mama, do you have any more furry fabric?" asked Mr. Michtom.

"Yes, I do," answered Mrs. Michtom. "And many, many more shiny black buttons, too."

Authors' Note

In 1902, President Teddy Roosevelt was hunting in Mississippi. He saw a small abandoned bear. President Roosevelt raised his gun to shoot the helpless bear, then changed his mind. He could not shoot the little bear.

His decision changed history. The rescued bear was the inspiration for America's most famous bear: Teddy Bear, named after President Teddy Roosevelt.

Cartoonist Clifford Berryman drew President Roosevelt saving the life of the baby bear. Berryman's cartoon was printed in newspapers throughout America.

One reader, a Russian immigrant named Morris Michtom, saw the cartoon. This sparked his Teddy Bear creation.

Michtom and his wife ran a small candy and toy store in Brooklyn. They loved children and children loved them. The bear President Roosevelt saved reminded Mr. Michtom of the toy Mishka bears of Russia.

The Michtoms made a furry bear with arms and legs and shiny black buttons for eyes. The Michtoms' bear looked like the one Teddy Roosevelt had spared.

They called their bear Teddy Bear in honor of President Teddy Roosevelt.

The Michtoms put their first Teddy Bear in their store window, where it was admired and quickly purchased. The customer was so eager and the sale was made so fast that Mr. and Mrs. Michtom made more of their Teddy Bears. Folks flocked to their shop to buy every bear the Michtoms made.

Mr. Michtom began to worry that President Roosevelt might object to the use of his name for a toy. So he and Mrs. Michtom made a very special Teddy Bear.

It resides today in the Smithsonian National Museum of American History in Washington, D.C. They sent their bear to President Roosevelt with a letter asking his permission to name it after him. President Roosevelt replied that the Michtoms were welcome to call their bears Teddy Bears after him.

And the rest is history!